WHIZZ IN ECSTASY

SUMEET KUMAR

Copyright © Sumeet Kumar
All Rights Reserved.

This book has been published with all efforts taken to make the material error-free after the consent of the author. However, the author and the publisher do not assume and hereby disclaim any liability to any party for any loss, damage, or disruption caused by errors or omissions, whether such errors or omissions result from negligence, accident, or any other cause.

While every effort has been made to avoid any mistake or omission, this publication is being sold on the condition and understanding that neither the author nor the publishers or printers would be liable in any manner to any person by reason of any mistake or omission in this publication or for any action taken or omitted to be taken or advice rendered or accepted on the basis of this work. For any defect in printing or binding the publishers will be liable only to replace the defective copy by another copy of this work then available.

Sumeet Kumar

Sumeet Kumar , A adult who experiences many phases of life , a well known writer and a writer of new era . In reality he is a writter as well as singer (as a hobby) and a standup comedian . Very exciting and interesting fact about him is that he is author of New era i.e. he starts his journey of writing at the age when he was going to schools to get the study . His streak of 100 books will be the great achievement for him in future. His some famous works i.e. Maturity Of Love (Genre - Love),Privacy For Dream (Genre

- Middle Class), Army Squad ofLove (Genre- The Seperation of Army Love), 5 Days of Love(Genre-Temporarily Love), The Endearment Of Love(Genre - Historical Era Of Love), Social Destruction Indo-Pak (Genre - The Story of The Love At The Time Of Division Of India And Pakistan), Middle Class Soul (Genre - The Dreams of Middle Class), The Accursed Kanatpur (Genre -The Horrific Story Of A Village), Wrong Number (Genre -The Suspenseful Physco Killer Story), The Secrecy OfDeadly Midnight (Genre - The Suspense About a Crime),Fragile Religious Of Death (Genre- The Death Of A TrustfulPerson), Nature Vs Science (Genre - The Future Battle Between Nature And Science In A Horrific Way), Generic Man (Genre - The Dream of I.I.T), The Unconsious 12 Hours(Genre - The Illusion At Stage Of Comma), The StrangeBurden (Genre - The Burden Of Love) , Her Existence (Genre- The Female Pain In The Society) , Jockstrap Prize (Genre -The True Story Of A National Athlete) , H Man [Hindi] (Genre - Superhero Tragic Story), H Man [English] (Genre - Superhero Tragic Story) , Maturity Of Love [Englsih] (Genre - Love) and many more are available on various geners on the offcial platform of **Amazon, Flipkart and Notionpress**. You can buy them from there.

Contents

Acknowledgements

Aman Kumar

Special Thanks to **Aman Kumar** who worked so hard in the preparation of this book. He has continually put with my passive voice, omission of words, and late night calls. You have been wonderful. Thanks to him for his precious time in reviewing proposals , individual chapters and early drafts, along with his suggestions on the applicability of the material to the world.

I

The Trauma of Tradition

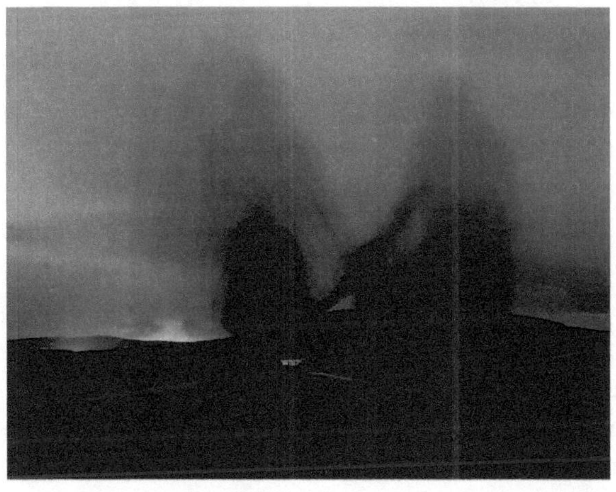

Life is such a train, whose track takes us every peacock
foot, where we try to meet everyone, we do batis and we

also screw ourselves with the things of the past, even if no one remembers these days, what should they do in the future They know very well that their feet feel sorry for the times, no matter how bad the condition may be, when the shadow of bad times comes, they take that saree to China with happiness, have you ever wondered how to live undefined Why nowadays it is said that after winning the people , running behind the job, running behind the wealth, running after the relationship and running after some people who do not respect you, do not call it living, do not give up such a life because This life is not the cost that we are facing, even if sitting on the grave foot, who asks that my fear will finally be buried Not talking about where people break and find themselves in a situation where even a long life is short in part. It seems and is full of pain, I will not share it, because only those who run away from their past, repeat their past, some people have curvy feet, what is their fault, because the fault is ours, I should write this in praise of it. There is such a dualt which is uncountable, the foot in the part does not belong to anyone, its love is also strange because the evidence which is already ruined it ruins it and good health, they say " Better undefined wastes the body, by the way Earlier in my childhood, I used to think and wish to grow up I wish I could get that, wish me this, I wish I could get long, wish me a house in Disney land, I wish a tsunami came. And after my school gets swept away in it, then I will get a leave for life, I used to think so much that life has turned the tables in reverse, in my childhood, when I used to watch cartoons like in Doraemon also I used to think that I wish man Not only did I think that there should be such a witness in my life, but at the same time, everyone thinks today.

feet, my story is not different from them, feet are not like them, dreams were big, feet were not expected, all the time used to promise to do something It was completely different, everyday used to dream such dreams which could never be fulfilled, it is not such a thing that did not dare It was wrong, in childhood, when someone made a mistake, dad and mom would come together to scold me, on one hand, papa would have saved me, and on the other hand, mom would listen to me and why did she not play by watching undefined? Maybe his scolding was also a love for me at some point, I can never forget those memories, saying that everything is fine, all the relationships I handled, with time, they came to my part and got tangled, people say. Everyone says that I am fine, nothing has happened to me, the legs keep breaking with disrespect, they feel the pain every day in the happiness that is clearly visible on their face, and on the other side they would log Whose pain is clearly visible on their face and feet and other people also understand that they came only after suffering the trouble of enough two or three and their face and feet are such that they have been suffering some pain in their part since many years undefined that of some people. There is love who expresses his pain to everyone and on the other hand there are some logs who never try to take away their pain from their share because with time it becomes their friend. In where the friends are weakening them even more, even after knowing these things, they do not ask them to leave the pain. Nowadays people often say hi in love. It is that I forget him, I say that I cannot forget my feet then it is an equal share, why is my leg missing and different why is this me taking my leisure undefined How can a girl forget her, in the world you can destroy someone's friends only when it is famous in your mind that your hatred is no longer present in her part, hate never ends love because with time it Tries to grow it further, and increases it to such an extent that even after saying it, she cannot forget it, drink it by mixing poison in water May be, life will take your time even when the age is raw, to understand that someone's love also seems to be a waste and it is also true somewhere, man For a witness, we forget the whole world, friends forget our dreams and in many surgeries, whose money is not going to take away from me by writing a donation, the result is that his friends are still imprisoned by me. In part and it is also that he is happy in his part with someone else and I am missing in my part, every one has prayed in part and in every mosque gurudwara . I have gone to the temple, I have not found his love in the foot part till today because no parent can ever see their children in any pain, nor can they give them such a waste in the part which they can not bear, thousands of times themselves These things were said that it is not wrong, what I am thinking, what I have done, what has happened to me is wrong, feet cannot be wrong, the moments we have played together, gave each other all the time That too in trouble, have taken care of each other, are of batis, have lade many times those words and those sarees, how can they be different? I have lost that love to her where my hair is not allowing me to live now, it is not a matter that now that love is over for her, even if the feet are in her part, why is this question always self-esteem. Why am I asking who is the right thing, who is trying to ruin me by coming in my mind, can someone's love be a deception, after all who was rightly wasted In the part that she showed me the world of all her deceit, which I could neither understand nor could ever bear her memories, if she can be happy then why not me who did I do the right mistake Because of which my happiness and all those memories of my gathering have become dear to me, I can force myself to go closer to her. Maybe the legend of the grave and the pain that I can't bear any more, maybe it is found in my part everyday, this whole life seems blurry now, who am I and why am I going to say enough, do someone's world axis is the right foot? undefined Can't she be happy in her life? Maybe she was suffocating her because of my compulsions, which I had expressed to her, maybe she could not stay with me in the journey and maybe she was trying to go through my journey with me, maybe everything was right And I was wrong. Why was my angry foot telling me that you can never be wrong Because I had never even thought that I do every single thing with whom I have gleaned my whole world, I say it to him, I remember every time to say that those moments are of happiness, these are of sorrow, If ever the feet collided with any floor. There is a question in my mind that I will definitely ask him, that after all, some pain is recommended on my part, even after saying it, I can not hurt myself, I feel alone in the evening and as soon as the night falls Your friends give me the freedom of those desolate abuses, which I am unable to separate myself even after saying it, if I had to ruin then why didn't you do it to someone else? Why did you get it? The pain that you have given me, I cannot cure it myself, because in the male part, I am not involved in anything. To come to the part, God used to recommend to him, he used to deprive himself of himself, what to say now, I do not understand because whatever charity I am writing in my part, I may be missing more by coming to your friends. Is it necessary to break my love that I should hate the love with which this whole world runs, why did you show dreams which could never be fulfilled with you, I knew that you could not support so long Even though I was aware of every pain, I still used to prove myself wrong by coming to your feet I am becoming known, you have decided in this way and I know your words too, these conversation undesirable yet My heart doesn't understand that now maybe we can't be the same as before, you are different, I'm different too I wish no one else could find his place in my place.

"I am not near you but i am around you
You are not with me but i am with you
I am wishing to be with you
You are not suitable for a wish says by god of
heaven but still i am wishing you
If this is the last birth of mine in this earth
I only want to be a lover of you"

II
Memory of Dark Mortals

It is said that there are some roads which are different from the floor, due to the nature of walking those feet, we get those moments of peace, even after saying that we can never try to erase it from our mind, nowadays everyone's enough to say that how to move forward in the world How to move forward Let's go because the life they are living is not enough for them I mean to say that if every day starts the same then we will never forget the morning prayer You may find that she is wrapped in pain, it is in the rays of peace, the witness about which I am going to tell you all, her life is a mystery and why is that, maybe you all can be aware of it in the bailout of time. Some such conversation are also incomplete in which part I have written, the feet have not yet been expressed in words, everyone has dreams, everyone has their own destination, there are dreams, distances are also there and love is the only thing. Don't do it, his nature is such that person often forget even themselves. Ordinary life becomes a puppet, neither all its threads are scattered and somewhere they are tied in such a knot that they can be opened, no one can try to open them because they are not used to it and Even if there was a habit, then his love would not let him live, if we walk on the road, then we see before our steps and after the road, that means the shadow that we make close to us, we see it first and the path which we have taken. undefined what is the difference between the two feet in its destination It goes wrong when we know that we can never get it Even after being successful, some people do not stop looking for something, but love is also a good thing. There is some mercy, they also have a different fate, which is very different from the rest of our hands, if there is strength in love, then perhaps every incomplete word of it can be fulfilled, saying that one sided these two durfs, in life Many people, we meet, we do conversation , feet are just a of that person which we accept a lot for a while That thing is never going to be found in luck, who is the right force behind it, which takes us closer to the place of keeping away from our destination, even if our feet are incomplete, yet we still get the good luck that we give to ourselves.

Everyday we ask for luck in the feet, perhaps his words are very different from our words How can it be that even if this thing happened, it could happen because neither I have completed my lamps yet nor the desire to see my dreams is incomplete. Right foot of desires complete .

Well the journey that I am about to start has started with a small girl where there is a different love story which is probably already famous. Each other's fate was very different, it was not just a story, it was a story, such an immortal story, which neither I can add to the story nor can I request to write its share in my share, because like their bailout It was also for each other, she was very different and very beautiful too, well we are not going to lose our way because the beginning is toh, Bazirganj, neither there story has started with a girl child nor grandson because she has not yet Continuing, because I am going to share my memories with her friends and that innocence of childhood, which with time had turned away from her for a while, feet, they say that changing the way does not change the destination, sir. By the way, the hero of our film is none other than Vikas Singh and his heroine is Kusum Yadav, both of them started the love story when our love story started. Nayak was fighting such a battle in his life that every boy of the village fights, don't understand the meaning I mean to say job sir, nowadays even the wood of city is at the forefront of hope, even after having a degree, he should never open a tea shop. If it has ever been of peanuts, it is not going to share this government of the society at the time, because many people have distributed about it and many people have also found this and many people have also got happiness because of this The story of victory does not tell you all to know because it is not just a unemployment, it is the feeling that today every youth feels and shares with art, fights feet, life leaves them with happy hope, where to return to life. many nights was memorable at the foot but the strength to move forward with the same hope is only one and that is only effort, well it is the beginning of time, it is the story of the teacher, toh kahliye phir seh do a new beginning means the one who tells in those childhood memories. Am who was maybe a little good and a little bad too, by the way, the beginning of the story has started on 12 August 2002, which means talking about the hero.The gift of getting them was written since time immemorial, because Vikas was born on this day, that means the fate of every child is decided on the day that it is going to be made in the future. They don't need any support, because they decide their dreams themselves and give birth to an expectation whose flight is very long, Vikas never thought that in the age in which he supposed as a protection was his desire also asks for the desire to move forward with the times, Vikas's dreams were not big, his hopes were big, he had never thought that he would leave his village and leave his home and leave his yards in such a way. Feet will go where the beginning of the floor is difference then , maybe his foot is the depth of the relationship, then the time breaks down, Vikas used to be a middle class family, that meant the four walls of the house were toh the feet of dreams, nothing special, with time How did his age increase and how did his studies become complete: he had not even lost his news in those childhood memories, so he was safe from his future. It had become difficult too, before trying to understand something, his dreams had become like the Taj Mahal, which we can only see, we can never call it our own, like this puzzle was the beginning of him when he left his singing and that too find

, I had come to Patna, where his feet lived with his relatives, he fulfilled his dreams at the time, which meant that he had to earn money at the time, he had fulfilled his feet. , Means when a person himself asks to move forward and do something, then the entire male time is present for his female feet, we cannot call him happy at the time, he is a waste that comes in the part and stirs up such an enmity.

Gives shelter in whose spirit the person forgets even himself, in the beginning, when he kept his house in Patna, he used to do small jobs, that too in the medical field, which he got with the help of his relationship Daro was hard work. His passion and his feet were not moving forward, that means he was not able to fulfill his dream, because when a girl grows up, then the mother becomes You say to get his sari done soon They do not live, even the walls of the house are tied to their duty, whose charity is very difficult for your home It is the joy of childhood in which I have seen my dreams, I have not fulfilled my feet, I have to fulfill them and become a successful person, that too in the eyes of the society, we are tied on a happy day. Leaving his home, he came. Vikas's dreams were similar when he had said goodbye to the abuses of his songs and his havoc, he had forgotten his childhood from the happy day and had passed at an age where he had lost his life. His family was nothing, it's not like his parents had demanded money from him, when our feet feel angry, neither are we At the same time, he takes care of himself in the debate and tries to go ahead with the debate, he did the same, day and night mango and night again his studies, in the same way he had given his 12th boards, that too from the arts stream, neither did anyone There was a degree that at that time he could work in a good hospital, the small things that he used to do by staying under a doctor, he did this work for many years, tried to move himself forward for his family too. Helped and kept giving profession to his parents also, then such a time also started in his life, whose reality forced him to leave the school now and start looking for more work, first trouble Initially, he was married to his father, who had an accident, which meant that he was the only man to manage his house at the time, because all the professions Vikas used to get was spent in him, that means in food and in paying the rent of the house, that means he is not that much help. Was able to do as much as he should have done in a happy time, after all, the second trouble that came to his family was none other than covid-19, which lasted all the time. There was an alarm bell for the country, after all, his father's job also went away and money also stopped coming, after all, household expenses, pressing professions and many more were such troubles which many people had suffered logs, the job of the impostor was not lost because he used to work in the medical sector for a while, he left that too for some time then he worked in a small home clinic as a caretaker, which gave him two benefits and a gift, Of money and other experience.

After all, after working for many years, his job was found at such a place where the beginning of a city on the banks of mother Ganges which is called Banaras and also the beginning of every love story of Kusum and Vikash.

"*I don't have any wish for making my dream a reality*"

But i accepts everything which is in reality
Loving you is a one sided wish in reality
But i invests my whole soul and energy for you in
reality"

III

Love in Dim

Not everyone's life is beautiful and not everyone's
dreams are fulfilled In the batiob karu, nowadays my pages
also start with a witness, which I had told , about the pure
intensity well there are some words in which we get lost in
our feet, sometimes they are never there, that means their
world is one.

I mean to say crime is recommended only by these feet, and aunt's saying is written in someone else's part, why am I saying this in the foot undefined because it has also been needed? It has been written in the gift that the age of Banaras and the love are two different lives, their principles are different, their dreams are different and their intensity is also applicable because as long as they feel life is incomplete and when they are completely in love So despite being pure, we do not do what he says, some things also happen like this. People from whom people become aware and try to understand a lot, in the end, his fear is also buried in the tomb like a mystery, and perhaps the condition of the one side where Vikas started his life is also like this They were meant to be completely different, perhaps they were like this, so let's go on this journey in which many logs forget themselves, forget their relationships, and enoughes put their whole efforts to get a witness. They never get that thing, doesn't it? Well, the last journey started on 6th November, that means when Vikas left the city too, where there was hope, his feet were not his dreams, so he came to Banaras to fulfill his unfinished dream. After all, what about Gaya Banaras undefined Banaras where Mother Ganga has that love, where people never consider and stay weak even after being weak, because a different relationship is associated, whenever the eyes open, only enough mother Ganga is seen in front, From the morning sun to the evening aarti, the love of mother Ganga is the only thing that touches her feet, when we forget all our sins, then happiness is such a son Justice started where the humanity of the human race still exists. When he left Patna and came to Banaras, he got his job, that too after many years of experience, where again he was seeing the benefits, one was money and the other experience. That, after all, even his dreams were unfulfilled, because when people leaves his work and his city, then I take his feet by any means, when his memories make us bereavement, then we will be happy for a while. The right feet forget everything, their duty, their dreams and their relationships, the condition of development was also similar because neither his friends he lived nor his family members had any relation, when the feet The dream is big, it seems to be small, even big troubles in front of them, and there were many such sari problems in its part, well they say that if you get the moments of peace, then someone's waste is also included in that and if in the part If we have got ruin, then moments of peace are also included in it, when no one is together, only then some people support and we take happiness together in the hope of living ourselves.and the steps in a relationship , friendship ,love and there was many such things are like, I can't even recommend saying. Dreams were also same means they both used to work at the same place, where they met for the first time in the heritage hospital and maybe after a few months it finally happened and how it happened undefined let us see when development When he got this job, he was very ignorant of Sushar Seh's abuses, he was jealous of her love and people's love too. Something like this became special, after which he forgot his songs, that meant his childhood memories, relationships and much more, he used to protect himself with her, listen to his daughters, even to fight with him, both of them For such a friendship was made for which he did not say to forget, maybe the beginning of one sided love is only a few words, I do not care because I Never did the feet, those who did it, the soul must now be saying how much you will suffer now, let's go ahead, so let's take the journey a little further and let's see what has happened in their future life? In the beginning, something happened that first they met each other, then they became friends, then they started working for each other and then fell in love and the story ends? Means if the story was like this, then maybe we also take it as one-sided. Love is like a dream, seeing which only we can feel two moments of peace, feet can never make it our love, feet whose dreams of many troubles in life were unfulfilled, so how is the beginning of his life full of dreams? Kusum used to live in such a family where her dreams were the only hope for her, meaning she was the only earner in her house, her father did not do any work, meaning she was unemployed, we do not consider her father wrong. The one who buried his dreams in the grave, made his daughter so successful that she could run the whole house on her own dam feet.

There was no other man in Kusum's house, meaning neither brother nor anyone was married because Kusum was the eldest in her house, she also had two sisters below her, whose names are Kritika and Preeti, that means she recommended some love. God said, where both of them are in the same condition, their dreams are completely different, the girl who did not obey her family, no matter what her condition, the debate went on and everyone kept fighting for her dream and herself. Before making success, the one who thought about his family, his luck can never be normal, nor can it be simple in the eyes of others because if I see him in my part, then his life is like a mirror, whose truth is also One side is not two sided, well Kusum had never told Vikas about his condition, nor Vikas had told his condition to Kusum, yet one-sided love had begun, that too in a gathering whose hope was deserted. Was and her story too, Wellish takes the story forward and sees what happened in their life when love on one side hurt their lives. At first, their meeting was quite simple, that means, at the beginning of the journey, when Vikas first came to Banaras and got the job of Oat, at that time he had only his own dreams, he was also moving ahead, at which time his meeting was not as much as Kusmu Seh. I know that when my feet met, my dreams changed too and I hope to ask Matt at some place because she was missing from the time of her life, by the way, I have not only said one thing, it is also necessary, I don't know. The feet may become necessary with time because when Vikas first came to Banaras, he was staying in Balaji Colony, close to the ground, where he got some friends, his dream started and somewhere their meeting also happened for the first time. I do not even know how true these batis are, then what like: When a new boy comes to school, we did not even allow him to sit near us and there is a reason behind this that many people are not in the place of our friend. In the right way, his life would have been the same if he had not met Kusum then, when they were in reality for the first time.when we met to each other on that time the conversation was nothing special between them, even after working at the same place, they were unknown to each other, you all know because as far as I have seen life is more No one's hatred for the bailout of time also lasts for long, meaning that one day his recommendations also go away from the mind when someone comes to love, both of them had no special feet for each other. Perhaps their friendship with time has finally happened, which means that those who were previously unknown were now able to meet each other, it means that there was a love-loving friendship between them, and maybe someone was in love on one side, then what was the month passed by? The friendship started getting deeper and perhaps the beginning of love was already over at the time, Vikash these daughters knew that she was in love, feet Kusum was very distant from it, I mean to say that she did not even know about the matter. She is understanding friendship, she has already recommended love on the other side, she could not tell her directly, I mean to say, the cafeteria she has.

She was facing the time, maybe she used to tell her not to apply at the time, meaning the app used to say not to come out of the undefined comfort zone undefined, she did not like only the baatis of safflower, with the passing of time, safflower also started liking her feet. They had forgotten that Kusum's condition would never accept her one-sided love, and perhaps their fate was also very bad for each other's share, after all, both of them had their friends on one side and Vikas's love on one side. After all, he had made it clear that he probably did not want to do it, his PK was also in the middle of his condition, why after spending many times with each other, they also separated from each other by doing Ahir in the gathering of friendship. They meant that Kusum had not come to the hospital for several days, which meant that her work feet were new and when both of them did not talk to each other for many times due to uneasiness, then after all, Vikash called those complete bags which might have been Kusum The man could not understand the time and perhaps even understanding his condition, he was forcing him to reject his love because on one hand his condition was too much. He was with her all the time, even though he was not in love with her, his feet were always near him, so even after saying no, his love story remained incomplete, where there was a writing on one side, luck was happy to get his feet on the other side.

After that, Kusum left that work as well, where her friendship was everything for her, now they do not work with each other and they only meet each other's love, Kusum is the love of foot development. For still it means only one sided and incomplete also undefined Well God will surely say that even if their unfinished story, even if the paper is incomplete, the feet may be accepted in reality, well the gut has been recommended if both of them If you meet then, perhaps the writing becomes complete instead of incomplete in luck.

"The luck of my heart is very nice
but luck of my love is not nice"

"Love is almost complete
but unfortunately is one sided
Every wish of forgetting her is almost complete
but unfortunately it is one sided"

9 7 9 8 8 8 7 3 3 2 7 2 7